THE
HUMAN BEING

A Warrior's Journey
Toward Peace
and Mutual Healing

STEVE MASON

A Touchstone Book
Published by Simon & Schuster Inc.
New York London Toronto
Sydney Tokyo Singapore

Touchstone
Simon & Schuster Building
Rockefeller Center
1230 Avenue of the Americas
New York, New York 10020

Designed by Deirdre C. Amthor

Manufactured in the United States of America

10 9 8 7 6 5 4 3 2 1

Library of Congress Cataloging in Publication Data
Mason, Steve.
The human being : A Warrior's Journey Toward Peace and mutual healing / Steve Mason.
p. cm.
"A Touchstone book."
I. Title.
PS3563.A798H8 1990   90-38455
811'.54—dc20   CIP
ISBN 0–671–66720–3

"The Casualty" from *Johnny's Song*,
Touchstone Books, Simon & Schuster, Inc., 1986.

"This Time, A Warrior for Peace" from *Warrior for Peace*,
Touchstone Books, Simon & Schuster, Inc., 1988.

I dedicate this book
to each who works to abolish war
so that the children of our world
may find the way to peace

Acknowledgments

Nobody does anything alone. It exists because of what others have brought to me. Thanks, then, to:

Richard Weidman who told me I should write (and kept telling me).

Patricia Hughes who fought (even me) for my words.

Jack Lyon who listened to every word almost as I wrote them.

Joe Benda who understood the words before I wrote them.

Mary Stout who gave me opportunity and courage to speak.

Don Weisberg who brought the message home.

Linda Cunningham who believed the truth.

Sol Skolnick who had the courage to say "yes" three times.

Carole Hall who steadied my hand and guided my pen.

Diane Franzone who held my other hand until it was done.

Dan Farley who said, "Let's do it right." And did.

Jan Scruggs who built "The Wall" where I made my vow.

Bill Mahedy because saving a man's life isn't something you should be thanked for only once.

HUMAN BEINGS ALL.

Contents

Part I

AT THE EDGE OF
THE WORLD

In the beginning, I was an American fighting man who fought and killed for the concepts of "duty, honor and country." Today, I am a man who has extended his citizenship to become a human being. I am still a fighter, yet I do not kill. I have become a warrior for peace and my commitment is to conscience, human dignity and the concept of one world.

MY HUMAN SOUL

My blood was born
long before I could bleed.
It knows, therefore, more about life
than my mind.
My sleek body sings
for fellatio & candy kisses,
while my confounded mind whines
about the possibility of a vengeful god
and the certainty of weapons testing.

But my soul, my human soul,
knows I am a human being
caught in the cross fires
of the Twentieth Century.
It cowers in the mud of my body
like I was a shell-hole
between the wars.

Sometimes,
I feel it look
from under the wires of my confusion
at the corporal madness
of this time and place—
knowing it wished we could be (together)
anywhere else.

It presses its mouth
against the glass of my eyes
(causing me a tear)

and utters the soundless scream
of a forgotten salamander
trapped inside a terrarium
on moving day.

THIS SELF

I was born
(this self with a name outside my blood)
with two gifts—
spontaneous laughter
and an even quicker sense
that the madness of this world
was unsafe for the innocent;
a death sentence for the brave.

By the time I could read I knew
that lunchtime turned the weak into meat.
And if a dreamer were to remain at the table
(instead of on it) he or she must be tough
and offer no smell to the mouth of power.

Later,
I would come to know
that "real life" begins
the first time you give up.
And that the concept of happiness
was not moored in the nature of this world—
that as close as I would ever come to joy
was the contentment of an atavistic revenge,
or the modern equivalent of a full belly,
an empty scrotum,
a boulder in the mouth of the cave
and a dream which did not wake the children
and send them running into the night.

I did not sit, therefore, on my father's knee
and tell him when I grew up
I would sell Lady Kenmores at Sears.

(ONE) WITH IT ALL ˙

There is a part of us (even as we live)
which is part of something greater.
A thing which outlives life.

You & I,
the old ones who went before,
the yet unborn,
are more than simple beings.
We are part of an evolving
collective consciousness—
a human spirit
beyond the rules of creaturehood,
outside the grasp of social order.
We are Human Beings,
one with it all;
each a part of what was,
(all) a part of what will be.

Certainly,
we have, one at a time,
been loved, lectured and beaten
by the reasonable people
and chaotic events of our lives,
but still we resist all attempts
to civilize our natures
and modify our truths.

We are substantially geographized,
nationalized, philosophized, uniformed,
shot-at, segregated and pissed upon,
but still we remain essentially,

what we showed-up to be—
human beings of a human spirit—
integrated within the concepts of Time & God;
inseparable from others of our kind
and committed to the secret world
of our small children
who share milk and cookies
(without being told it is good).

Truly,
you and I have much in common.
It is in our blood, it is in our souls;
we cannot be vaccinated or indoctrinated
against our humanity.
Not for any cause. Not for any reason.

It is to you, then, that I write.
It is like speaking to myself
above the roar of madness.

QUESTIONS AND ANSWERS

Like you,
I know a thing or two about life.
You know what I mean.
Not things like the quadratic formula
or *i* before *e* rules of grammar,
but things like life sucks and people stink.
You know—*real* things
a guy can use in a sentence
and everybody understands.
Wisdom.

And I got questions too.
Not about why people go to war
or who says Time moves in only one direction?
But questions about things you can't talk about—
like how come I can't really imagine a world
without me in it (and you can't either)?
Abstract questions. Intellectual.
You know the kind.

But answers?
Answers, I don't know about.

Maybe it's because
being a human being isn't like being
a peanut butter-and-jelly sandwich;
final and delicious.
It's more like being a monster and a god,
something terrible and creative;
powerful, generous and stupid.

And most of all growing.
A child-thing dancing at the edge of its world.

To believe in us we've got to believe
in a world of wonder and of evil;
to put our faith in a world
where everything is possible
and nothing is certain. Not even tomorrow.

As for me,
if there is grace in my life
it's because someone like you or you
has come into it.
Yet, every nightmare I've ever lived
has had one of your faces.

Hell, all I know about God
is what I trust humankind can become.
Yet, all I've ever seen of the devil
is what I know mankind to be. . . .

Yeah, I have some goddamned questions
for the answers I was fed as a child
about this unformed "us"
which rules a starving planet
and lives in fear of itself.

And there's nobody but you to ask.
So I write to you
and ask us in *all* my voices
the human questions our children always ask
until the age of three when the world stops
its perfectly spinning human acceptance of being
to pivot only on the rude lie of endless "yeses."

Writing to you
is like opening my soul to nine centimeters
and at the moment of greatest pain,
pushing down on the exhale
to create a screaming new truth
which sounds like both of us.
(Always at the instant of greatest risk
there is the sense of perfect clarity.)

It is the courage of our questions
which gives us the truth of our answers.

Part II

DAUGHTERS AND SONS

When I was forty years old, an unexpected and delightful daughter was born. She came into the life of this hard-bitten and snarling combat veteran like rain to a desert. For three years and two months I assumed the role of primary parent. It was like being born again. In introducing her to the world, I made peace with it myself. "Mothering" her remains the only thing I have ever done which made natural sense to me. It is she who encouraged me to see life in human terms, and she, therefore, who put the pen in my poet's hand. These days I see daughters and sons everywhere. I would give my life to make them free and safe. But I do not know how.

FLOWER

The Rex Hotel, Saigon 1966

She said her name was Flower
and she was right.
It was a "made-up" name,
but she was that kind of kid.
A six-year-old girlchild
on a wartime rooftop
looking out at the world
one night in the rain.

She was a little poem
in a big book about a war
we were both living at the time.
I got to be the lines
about the hard-core paratrooper,
she got to be the little verse about
what it was supposed to be All about.

We met there at dusk by accident.
Me to brood. Her to play.
We just happened in the same space
and had watched the sun set together.

A beautiful cherub with black bangs
sharp-cut at the arch of her eyebrows,
and eyes like bright coals
which caught the fire from the sun
as it went down

and seemed to dance as she spoke.
And she never stopped speaking.

The little sounds her voice made,
were the songs of the innocent.
So that while I was with her
and her rag doll named "Co"
(which looked so like her it was comical)
I felt not so tired,
not so old
and somehow, more like me than in months.
We laughed easily.

When it was dark
We held hands on the balcony
as I watched the flares
and felt the dull thumps
of the "other guys'" war
across the Saigon River,
knowing that tomorrow
I would return to mine.

She looked out
(from under the railing)
at what for her
was all she'd ever known
about life.
What she saw there
with those eyes
as big as wonder
I will never know.

I was a kind of a tourist.
She, a kind of a local.
Both of us (and all of it)

just passing through.
(God only knows to where.)

Just like "real life"
we got hungry at the same time
and had fun just inches
out of the cold monsoon rains
deciding in two languages
and whoknowshowmanygestures?
about what to eat on the ledge
and who would go get it.

She won
because she couldn't leave.
(Her mother would be off work soon.)
I lost
because I didn't want to break the spell.
We decided she would get two desserts.

The laughter and the music,
the smoke and the shouting
inside the officers lounge
as I opened the balcony door
to get us some chicken soup
and three pots de crème
chased me back out under the eaves.

I didn't belong in there.
The whole time I was in that fucking war,
I never felt comfortable with Americans.
Somehow they were not a part of my war.
I lived with the Vietnamese
in a village 140 kilometers
southwest of Saigon
along the Cambodian border.

I took my chances with them.
The Americans were my brothers.
But when I shared food or faced death,
it was with Vietnamese farmers.
They were my comrades.

The charts in MACV Headquarters
had my village colored in red—
under Viet Cong control.
I was up to give a briefing
which would not change the color
on the map that week
nor any other week
for as long as we kept the charts.

As I approached our playful place
Flower was peering over the roof
at some commotion on the street.
Suddenly, she leaned dangerously
through the wrought iron bars.

Sirens wailed as I called her name.
"Ba! Ba!" She screamed like a banshee.
I jumped to the railing
and pulled her to me.
She wrestled away from me
and darted to the exit—
the cry for her mother
piercing the rain and the night
like a tracer round
as she ricocheted
down the stairwell.

I grabbed at the railing
and jackknifed into the rain

for a quick look
at the scene on Tu Do Street
four floors below.

Two women were being dragged and carried
into a police wagon by the "White Mice"—
the white-helmeted Kanh Sat
of the Army of Vietnam.

A crowd of onlookers opened ranks quickly
and then closed tightly, as a third woman
ran into the busy intersection,
two "white mice" in pursuit.

A horn-honking jumble
of military and civilian vehicles
of every description
agonized in the downpour
to avoid hitting the woman.
Miraculously, she gained the other side
and raced toward the river.
Somehow I knew she was Flower's mother.
I began to root for her
as the Kanh Sat drew their pistols
and jostled into the resistant body
of the sidewalkers.

How sudden everything is about war.
How strange it is always the same—
one second, shared laughter;
the next, controlled panic.
The second after that, a cigarette.

Flower hit the street
just as I stuck a Pall Mall in my mouth.

She never stopped at the curb.
The black Renault taxi hit her full-on.
The impact lifted her high into the horizon.
My blurred focus picked out her mother
going down under the policeman
just as Flower was going up into the sky.

For one swollen moment,
the war
the city
the world
all hesitated—
paused at the brim of myself
like water hangs above the glass
a rounded edge before outpouring.

I knew she was dead
before she ever hit the ground,
one small flower plucked from my heart.

I picked the rain-soaked tobacco strands
from the blood of my lips
bent down for the fallen rag doll
and holding it in both arms
went back to join the party.
The bass drum
and the dull thumps became one. . . .

MIDNIGHT IN BELGRADE

Teary little girl
in layers of clothes,
where is your mother?
And why do you cry so,
alone at midnight
in Belgrade?

Have you no doll to hold
as you wander the tracks
of the train station?

I wish I could hold you.
It is so cold
and the big people
are rioting in the city
or hiding like the dead.

If I knew what language
you spoke, I could not speak it,
but still I would hold you.
For you and I
and all the night around us
are all alone and all we have is us.

See there, little seven year old,
that official who ignores you?
He, too, is afraid and no doubt
has lost *his* mother long ago
one night as cold as this one.
He is not afraid.
See how he passes you by

as if tears and loneliness
meant nothing if the train
is only on time?

Do not cry so.
See here, under the blankets—
the white-whiskered gypsy women
who smoke and crouch in the shadows
waiting for nothing to take them slowly
to nowhere in the morning?
They will help you. Come take my hand,
they know everything and always have.
We will ask them with my cigarettes to help.
Surely, old women know the way of lost girls.

Ah, see, the gnarled-handed one with black lips
speaks to you and takes my pack of Camels.
She will help you (but do not use her handkerchief).
And I will follow not too closely
to see that you again are loved by someone special
and not just everyone as I.

And should this train now pulling in
(longer and more lonely than the rest)
which goes this night to Russia,
leave without me, still I will stay with you.
And if that one which left before
for some place in Romania, have your mother on it,
we will go tomorrow and will find her.

Oh, little one,
this night you are the world to me
and all that's right and wrong with it
and I know that of all the ones I could not save

in all the other lives I've lived before you,
there was not one (so like them all) as you.

Oh, little girl, who runs just now
into her mother's arms, I cannot tell you
how much it means that you turn to me and wave.
I did not know you noticed I was alive and cared.

BRING *ME* YOUR BABIES

There is no wind I cannot breathe;
there is no salt I have not eaten.
I am a man whose mother loved him;
I consume my world like good food.
(I was taught that I belong here.)

Yet there are those who vomit life
like they were allergic to it all.
They fight for breath in the crib
and live anemic lives until death
drains the need to suffer further.
(They have no sense of beingness.)

There is no such thing as a lover
who is not a gentle giving parent;
sex is foreplay to birthing gods.

Who would let himself be fondled
by a woman who beat his children?
Where is the woman who loves *him*
who would violate his daughters?

When in the throes of "la petite morte"
(that ecstatic eruption of creaturehood),
the horrible vastness of exact beginning
is enlightened by a paroxysm of rapture
in a breathless groking of life & death.

Banging in black and thrusting rhythms
of endless truths and immediate orgasm,

the moment of precise creation prevails
in a near perfect replication of lovers.

It is a fixation of unquestioned "is"—
when she&you, you&he, ups & downs and
god & time and all our days and nights
skip like a smooth rock on a dead pool
to stutter-step into a drowning bubble
at the bottom of liquid spinning space.

From such ends, such as we begin again.
Our world waits to be created each time
by the brave new dreamers who come to it.
We need only to welcome them and nurture
them and the cosmos finds new meanings.

If you find this place too cruel to live,
if you cannot bring joy to the children,
then I clench the fist of my human soul
and howl from the mouth of all our gods,
"Bring *me* your babies, I will raise them!
I can raise the world, because I am loved!"

FATHER! FATHER!

"Father! Father! I your son!"

They are jubilant and sweaty—
two street kids in their late teens.
One black. One white. Both yellow.
All smiles.

"Father!" the black kid pants.
"Take me home!"
He stops too close to me.
He smells like garbage and flowers.
I hug him to me
and reach a hand behind him
to his hard-breathing friend.
"Thank you, Father," the white kid says.

The black kid is a beautiful young man,
chisel-featured with soft, almond eyes.
He fishes out a dog-eared photo of his dad.
It is a black-and-white snapshot
of a teenaged soldier with a smile
like he won the lottery.
"His name is Lucas.
You will find him for me?
I want go U.S."

The white kid is a straggle-haired,
rat's-ass mess who seems brain-damaged.
He, too, has a photo.
His father's name is Larry.
I have as much chance

of finding their fathers
as we do of being struck by a meteorite
in the next five seconds.

The Amerasians are called
"The dust of the world."
Unloved, unwanted, uneducated,
unemployed and mostly homeless.
All of their fathers long gone.
Most of their mothers long dead.
To the Vietnamese government,
these children are the embodiment
of the American rape.
Girl children do what they can to survive.
Boy children can do even less.
Many of the most unfortunate
sleep together in a city park
for mutual protection.
Evil swarms over them like flies on refuse.
If Vietnam is the "third world,"
these children of God
live in the fourth.
And if there are heavens, each will have one.

On earth,
I make them the wealthiest Amerasians
in the city and say good-bye.

I feel like scum.

SOMETHING *I* CAN SING

Harry Chapin is dead.
The children are still hungry.
I'm a bag. Bush is President.
Tonight the children of Nicaragua
will do their homework,
maybe study English.

For some who died this month
it's suppertime three weeks ago.
It's not time yet, in Cambodia.
This Man God is Everywhere.
So I'm certain there's been no mistake.

I wonder sometimes if god was ever little
and if he ever missed a meal.
Wonder too,
what he thought of the prayers from Auschwitz
and if he ever spent Christmas in a trench.

You know what I mean.
I mean did God go to OCS
or was He born with His star?

Harry Chapin's dead.
I'm still alive.
The children are hungry.
There must be Something *I* can sing.

SOMETIMES AT NIGHT

Sometimes at night
I lie with this woman
who has opened twice her thighs
that I might see two infant faces of god
and kiss her cheek as she arcs her hips
to lift me gently into sleep.

But sometimes (like tonight)
nature cannot tranquilize me
against the final screams of *distant* children
who fight for breath and die from hunger
far outside the door of *my* little dreamers
snoring-off their porkchops and their Twinkies.

Like you, I love them all.
The ones I hold,
the ones I will never meet.

Ours is a human family.
My nation has no enemies
whose children I would not raise as my own.
They are all *our* children.

Under this pale moon
I cannot sleep counting sheep.
The night breath of wolves smells of babies.
I hold my ears against the crunch of little dreams.

Part III

SISTERS AND BROTHERS

*Any meaningful conversation with one's self is a dialogue
of conflict and resolution. Often, the voices seem to come
from more than one person. But by accepting the diversity
within ourselves, we become better able to accept the
differences between each other. One of the joys of being
human is to embrace multitudes. To make peace with one's
self is to make peace with the world.*

ANRIE

I

When God exits East Berlin
through Checkpoint Charlie,
She takes no pictures
and descends upon Paris
through the dome
of the Cathedral of Notre Dame
(avoiding the pickpockets).

Quasimodo does not ring the bells
(except in my ear) but the gargoyles play
on the ramparts of all our earthly fears.

Superstition and intuition
bind visitors to the outdoor benches;
religion glues the devout to the inner pews.
Each lights a candle
before the dark window of her or his soul.

Satisfied,
She inhales the pork and lentils
in a side-street restaurant in Saint-Séverin.
She agrees, it is a miracle!
In this, God and I are as one.

II

I come here a stranger without language.
A visitor, not a tourist.
A traveler, not a pilgrim,

I scurry the late night alleys of D'Artagnan
searching for courage and innocence and truth
finding only the grim mornings of Richelieu.

I discover by accident the place on the quay
where Inspector Javert removed his greatcoat
and plunged into the Seine to drown his guilt.

The literature of my youth pours out of Paris
like wine down a gutter
in the Province of Burgundy.
Dumas is here. Hugo is here.
Descartes, Rousseau, Voltaire. Hemingway, too.
Romantics, realists, existentialists, egotists,
opportunists and assholes. All here.

Yet, my intellect picks up a rock
and runs to the barricades.
There is something wrong here.
This is not the Paris of Ho Chi Minh;
neither is it the Paris of my youth,
nor of the people I have read.
It is sixty years too late for that.
I get depressed.

God goes, perhaps, to hold up Mars
and to watch the morning
come over the hills
and onto the fields of Cambodia.

III

I say to hell with it
and take Hemingway to bed
in a small (manly) hotel

surrounded by old churches,
narrow doorways and succinct cafés.

It is in my fiftieth year
that I read Hemingway
this macho night
in first edition.

For the first time
I understand Papa.

For Whom the Bell Tolls,
written when I was born,
cracks sharp into my eye.
Its dry spine breaks
into brittle crumbs
of black truth onto my lap.
In my own mind I think,
it is good to be in Paris
and to be with Hemingway.
But I am not a young man.
And I am not here to write.
Nor to read. But to feel.
It is too late to grow up.
Too late to be a student
or an excited dilettante.
I am a fucking adult male
walking around my world
to get a glimpse of myself
while it still matters to me.

God knows I am not a suicide.
Yet,
the bodies of dead young men,
caught on the wires of *my* war,

grin back from only one face
under the nightly searchlights
of conscience and of guilt.
Their human blood long dry
on the faded, acid pages
of international newspapers
like cum on the stiff sheets
of a payday's whore.

IV

I am not comfortable in this room.
Suddenly, I need life and light.
Paris is still the City of Lights.
I dress quickly, yet with impeccancy
and go again into the streets of Paris.

I see her as I gain the lobby.
She sits on the divan
like a self-portrait
waiting for a wall on which to hang.

She is alone in the beauty of herself:
Monied, cultured, confident.
As I approach, I see now she is not alone;
tragedy sits with her on that divan
like it bought the clothes she wore.

I love life
and beauty does not discourage me.
Nor, for that matter,
does fragility entice me.
I remain within myself—

a man gifted with appreciation
and cursed with a sense of mischief.

I stand before the cathedral
of this rare beauty's need
and smile a "Yeah, me too," smile
as she notices my fighting weight
is draped in Italian silk
and that my eyes (like hers)
are a little sad, but somehow unafraid.

We speak
(I do not remember the accident of words).
Her English is studied, her manner light.
We leave together to find *her* Paris.

We walk the Left Bank
in a drizzle-ridden,
late night fog.
I tell her I do not love Paris—
I loved Saigon too much
to ever love Paris.

I explain,
a system which sustains such beauty
by exacting such pain elsewhere,
is itself an ugly thing.

I say something else
in a clever pejorative
about Parisians.

She laughs, sort of.
A Japanese, Russian laugh
with a French accent.

V

We are in front of the 5-star hotel
where the release was signed
for the concentration camp internees.
She tells me, leaning into an archway,
how war in Europe and war in the Far East
forged the marriages in her family
that have her dreaming of world peace
as a Russian, Japanese, French woman
working as an international actress
living in England where she sifts scripts
looking for roles which let her speak the truth.

I do not hear her particularly.
I am absorbed by her face and her tears.
My mind tries different combinations
of genetic overlays and history maps
to match her face with the times and places.
I give up quickly. She is a human being.
It is enough.

I listen in distant terror
to the tales of her relatives.
It is like listening to my sister
speak of my own family.
It seems strange to me;
I do not recognize the names.

We walk, she rearranges my raincoat
over my shoulders; we do not misstep.

She speaks of a relative in Russia
trapped at the outbreak of war.
I think of my grandfather, age 11,
running across the frontier
his whole world on fire behind him.

She speaks of a Japanese grandparent
and cries at something unuttered
about the atomic bomb.
It begins to rain hard.
Her mascara runs. We do not.

I think of the first time
I saw my mother cry;
President Truman said over the radio
the day "we" dropped the bomb,
"We thank God
that the atomic bomb has come to us
instead of our enemies,
and we pray that God will guide us
to use it in His way and for His purposes."
She wrote it down when I was five.

Over espresso and cognac,
this lady talks of her friend, Marcel Marceau,
and lightly, about other greats she has known.
I am underwhelmed.

She speaks of France.
I am incensed.
Liberty. Equality. Fraternity.
Tell it to the Vietnamese!
I saw French colonialism
up-close and personal.
Saw it in the jungles of French Indochina

where they had chained the children
to the trees in the rubber plantations
and later (after sitting-out WWII)
where they tried to retake it
(with American dollars)
from the nationalists who had fought
the Japanese and revered the words
of Abraham Lincoln, finding alliance
only with the communists which American boys
again had to fight for the French.

Sure, I think the Louvre is peachy-keen,
but frankly, I prefer the sidewalk artists
who scribble in charcoal outside the museum.
Their art is not a part of the institution
and, therefore, makes clumsy weaponry,
unlike the designers of the Exocet missiles
fired into British warships
by Argentine dictators,
later found guilty of crimes against humanity.
(I make no sense, but it is the truth.)

Lafayette, we are here! My ass.
And we're still here. Supporting NATO
with sixty percent of U.S. defense budget.
Don't talk to me about the French.
And the trouble with Paris is the Parisians.

She is delighted.
(What am I to do with her?)
We walk back to the hotel;
she talking incessantly
about speaking the truth,
about people, about war,
about peace, in her work and in her life;

me, eating a pound of assorted French pastries,
saying nothing while loving the best of Paris.

I know everything and nothing about this person.
I have never been more comfortable with anyone.

In an arched doorway
we find shelter from the downpour.
I strain my eyes to read
the small, bronze plaque
inset above the doorbell.
It is for a young man named Henri
who gave his life one night
in this side street,
a hero of the Resistance.

She waves her hand to embrace the night sky
as if in wonder or in question or in plea
and tells me of that time in Europe
when the world was no more cruel than now,
but was so perfectly ordered
that the finest medieval minds
devoted their lives to the question of their Age:
How many angels could dance on the head of a pin?

We both look up and then to each other.
In the line at the corner of her mouth,
Michelangelo would have died forever.

At the hotel
we say good night like old friends and lovers
for whom tonight is not a nervousness.

When we say good bye two days later,
it is with separate notes left in our boxes.

I go to Germany, she to England,
each a little sadder than before.

Poor Anrie,
who has no identity
except with us all.

LADY M

Nothing, not even penmanship,
or a high note on a flute
is as neat as a London flat.

I enter the home of Lady M
and step inside a greeting card,
handmade exclusively for Harrods.
The signature of herself
moves like calligraphers' ink
across the imprint of the room
in a quick and certain stroke
to the dot of her i
above a pastel sofa.
It is a perfect appointment.

I think,
if I could reach both walls
and open wide my arms,
her life would pop up
in three dimensions
from the middle of the room.

She speaks.
Cardboard disappears.
Her words are the music of today.
Life springs from out the room
with all the power and wonder
of a sidewalk flower.

By a window over the flower garden,
I sit before this gentle lady

of unimaginable courage
and inestimable strength
and feel as insignificant
as a thumbprint on a vase.

I know that just here, in this chair,
sat Nelson Mandela in 1962.
I know that just there, in that sofa,
sits his biographer.
She talks to me as if I am a real person.
I feel ashamed for not being invisible
like a fan in the after-game locker room,
some great player just offered champagne.

Lyrically, she speaks to me of her life.
It is like being read to aloud
from a picture book of the Iliad.
An aristocratic young lady
who knew the hedgerows and headquarters,
corporals and generals of World War II
and later dedicated herself
to fighting its causes
in the non-peace which followed.

From Europe to South Africa
she has fought the Nazi mentality
with her total complement of grace,
fearlessness, intelligence and commitment;
fought it with a single weapon: truth.
The same truth in which she addressed
the United Nations on apartheid.

The front pages of any daily tabloid
speak of the ground she has won
and the losses she has taken.

Her fight is our fight.
It is the good fight.
And she is a heroine.

Nelson Mandela gave a speech,
"Not an easy walk to freedom."
He has been in prison
for twenty-eight years.

Lady M has been banished
from her beloved country
where she was under house arrest.

Still, with bandages on her hands,
she writes the truth
which knows no boundaries
and without which no man,
no woman, no child, no place,
can ever be free.

Lady M is my friend
who serves me tea
from broken fingers
in the middle of day.

Mary Benson
is the poem
in a get-well card
to South Africa.

MARION

I

I get a kick out of my mind
watching itself like a four year old
in a mirror.
It embarrasses me to catch myself
playing dress-up.
Mostly, my mind plays
when it thinks I'm almost asleep
or too aggravated to care what it's doing.

It's not the same detachment
from which, sometimes,
I send it out ahead of me
like on some secret mission
and it waits on the side of a partisan hill
for me to parachute in with the equipment,
like when it waits for me on the back
of a little finger tracing the outline
of a new lover's cheek
when I notice that gesture
makes her smile in a sorry sort of way
and wonder (coming down) just how I knew
to do *that* just then
and my mind makes contact with me
and smiles, "I've waited here for 20 years,
I thought you'd never come."

II

No, it's more like that time
when I dozed staring out the window

of the train at dusk
into the corridor of land
by the railine in East Germany
and considered the farmland
when my mind took a walk
it didn't think I noticed.

I watched it look both ways
and start to fuck around
between the window and the hills.
It wondered
(while I watched the stunted fields)
whether it would rather
hit a home run
every time I came to the plate
in the fourth grade,
be a poet
or smother Hitler in his crib.

I was about to comment to myself
when it turned from its game,
jumped back into my consciousness
and hollered,
"She's coming! Quick, she's coming!"

I never doubt myself
and sat up fully alert
crossing my legs casually as she entered
the open compartment from the aisle
like a night breeze through gauze.

The most beautiful woman I had ever seen.
One of those thirty or forty thousand women
with whom I could have lived happily forever.

She smiled and nodded shortly as she brushed by
and turned to struggle her bag into the rack.
She was dressed in an ohmygod! black ski outfit
of that flesh-stretch material which outlined
her firm fitness like she was a nude fresco
on Hadrian's Wall.

But it was her face
which tightened my abdominals.
Made me wish she'd found
an empty seat in non-smoking.
In my life, not on any street corner,
not on any screen,
had I ever seen a more perfect harmony
of line and shadow,
character and unblemished beauty.

At the corner of her eyes was drawn
just the thinnest of lines to suggest—
no, to hint—that she had lived
and that the hugeness of those black eyes
had seen life and been opened wide
with the wonder of it,
so that when she looked at you
it was as if she had dreamed you
and when she turned away
you would wake dead.

"Oh,"
I said to myself looking up,
"NICE WORK, GOD!"
And said to her the cleverest speech
I could dry-mouthed utter
and addle-brained commit to memory,
"Hi."

She smiled,
adjusting herself in her seat
and was silent.
Silent as my falling ego
which had thought to impale her
with my now limp word.
A word which should have made her incapable
of off-handed movement and casual gesture.
It strikes me at that moment
what a jerk I am
and I laugh at me as usual.
Hi. Indeed.

Why not instead, the truth—
"Excuse me lady,
but would you think it presumptuous of me
to ask if you needed a slave?"
Shit.

III

OH Christ, my mind is glad I'm alive!
Happy to be here,
in the "now" of *this* reality,
knowing that this Polish train
railing across East Germany
is taking us to some unpronounceable world
where little gods with big bellies
wear lederhosen
and eat granola for breakfast.
A world where she and I
will step off into yellow fields
of wild and mad and free
to start a new species of children

who learn math and science
by somersaulting in clover and dew
and counting the dimples in their toes,
while she and I make love all morning
in the loft of a gingerbread barn.

That's it. I'm mad!
I'm outa' here!
I'm gonna bend over,
swipe an imaginary speck off my shoe
and some final, flashing thing
is gonna' explode in my temple.
I'm history.

Well, either that, or maybe,
I'll just sit here quietly, maturely,
ignore her until I get to Berlin,
dine with a chandelier over my head
and take a shit on Hitler's bunker.

IV

I force myself to look out the window
(away from her).
I tell my mind
to go play outside like before.
It refuses like a recalcitrant child.

The conductor, two armed guards
and a muzzled dog
appear in the doorway.
Ah, something I understand.

Predictably we argue. Who cares why?
They are always wrong.

And they love their work.
Great fun in any language.
Great fun without language.
They leave not feeling good
about this compartment.
I am delighted. Fuck them.

There is a light touch on my arm.
I turn slowly to her.
She sits diagonally across from me
and leans toward me
offering me a napkin-wrapped goodie
from her handbag.
I nod a polite thankyou
as she snaps the confection
with surgical skill.

She does not know
I would eat a live snake
if she offered me one.
I say, "Thanks, ladyfriend,"
in a measured, American way
with just a hint of continental casualness.
(I am delighted with me again.)
She tears the paper napkin
in such a way as to speak of years
doing without.
I realize at once she is sharing
all she has with me and wonder why.

She gestures with her head
in the direction of the guards
and shakes her head like her hair is wet.
Her nose (that gorgeous sculpted line of regality)
wrinkles like an Easter bunny and she says,

"No gudt."
I smile genuinely and agree, "No gudt."
She breaks into an upside-down clown smile
and wags her shoulders like a theatrical soldier.
We laugh as I stick out my tongue
and lean my head into the aisle
to give the boys a bronx cheer.

She tries to imitate it—
crumbs fill the air like sugar motes.
We laugh together; try to surpress it
and get a fit of the giggles.
We are like schoolchildren. It is delightful.

V

It is a full minute before the moment passes.
Her face is flushed, she is even more beautiful.
Our breathing returns to almost normal
when she makes a palms-up gesture and a shrug,
"No English," she explains.

I make the same gesture, "No German."
She pauses and asks with a pounce, "French?"
I shrug again. She tries again. And again.
I interrupt with mock enthusiasm, "Vietnamese?"
She says no seriously with her eyes,
thinks about it
and we get hysterical again.
God, I want to make love to this woman!

I make a show of cleaning my plastic glass
and pour her some white wine.
I start to say something slowly,

think better of it and for a moment
my mouth stays open like a retard's.

She tries to say something
and is similarly reminded.
We can't fucking speak to each other.
Shit.

We both start to speak at once.
We stop; look at each other expectantly,
hoping for a breakthrough.
There is none.
(Speaking just for me,
I think we should take our clothes off.)

I look away from her out the window.
My eye joins my mind
in the eaves of a thatched farmhouse
to watch the sunset.
My mind wants to stay there;
it is beautiful.
You better hurry up, shithead,
I say to myself, this train is moving!
My mind slips past the window ledge
and is gone from view—it wings back.
It scampers over the village steeple
and sails across the moon's face.
"I've got it! I've got it!"
You've got what, boo-boo?
And my mind jumps into the compartment
and whispers breathlessly into my ear,
"The pictures. Show her the pictures!"

I stand up and retrieve a leather notebook.
In an inside flap I remove a photograph

of my two young daughters.
I extend it to her. She beams.
Into her purse, out of her wallet—
the picture of her three sons.

We sit staring at the best of ourselves.
This is the reality. The fantasy is gone.
She is still beautiful,
but I do not desire her.
She is the piano I never learned to play.

VI

Her face composes a new softness
when she looks at me. She relaxes.
I wonder at the mechanism.
I look away—out the window again.
Asshole, I say to myself, jump out there
and tell me what it is that has happened.

That which knows
what I do not think, detaches,
but does not leave my consciousness.
It rummages through my experience
and holds up an old truth
like a pair of ballet slippers
from an attic trunk:

In the eyes of a man,
a woman loses her virginity
when she is married.
In the eyes of a woman,
a man loses his virginity
when he has children.
It is not personal,

it is natural.
A man is a boy who wants a woman;
a woman is a mother who wants children.

Each of us lives in a world
of our own truths.

In my mind,
this lovely lady and this hairy poet
can enjoy an infinite, human friendship;
one not bordered by our parents
on the one side,
and by our unborn children on the other.

The train stops somewhere near Düsseldorf.
It has a sinister name
from a World War II movie.
I look at the name painted in black,
sinister letters suspended on wires.
I look at the terminal for something
dark and dangerous.
It is just a train station.
I am disappointed.

VII

We are joined by two people;
a polite, young man in his early twenties
who struggles with a knapsack of books,
speaks English with an Indian accent
and who sits directly across from me,
and a matronly woman with a sinister limp,
who wears Himmler's eyeglasses
and carries an umbrella

which obviously conceals a sword
of Solingen steel.

The woman sits beside me,
across from my friend,
whom she immediately begins to question
in German.

The train passes a short wall.
lit by spotlights.
It is covered with barbed wire
and broken glass.

I comment in gallows humor
to the young man something
about not wanting to see
what was on the other side, anyway.

He says something in German
to our companions.
They mutter sadly.
The young man says
that what I would see
is terrible farming.

I encourage him.
He explains
that the finest earth in the world—
an airborne silt of perfect pH balance—
exists at a depth of hundreds of inches
in only three isolated places:
in Russia, in China, and here,
in East Germany.
Where it exists, collective farming
makes a mockery of growing food.
My mind tugs at me and says

this guy is a nerd.
A scholarly nerd, but still, a nerd.

The spy lady interprets him to my friend.
He continues, that he is an agronomist
getting his Ph.D in India;
that he has just finished his military
obligation by doing community work for a year
and is returning next week to India.

I asked what he did in the community.
He cleaned urinals
because he refused to enter the army.
His father is a businessman in Berlin
who was an antiaircraft gunner
in the Big War and whose partner is British—
a bomber pilot who made raids on the city
where his father served.
He loves both men
and is glad they joke
about being lousy shots
when they were young.

His father is proud of him.
I am proud of him.
He makes us all cry.
I say to myself,
this scholar is a tough man.
And no kind of nerd.

The matron says to me
in spy-school English
that the lady across from her
wonders what kind of work I do.

I tell her I am a poet.
It causes a tumult.
It makes me wish I wrote in German.

Ladyfriend asks spy lady
what I write about.
I say I write about war
and I write about peace.
Another tumult.

The three talk all at once—
to each other and to me.
I consider moving to Europe.

Ladyfriend says she lives in East Berlin
and her sons' names are Fritz (of course)
Jahne and Thomas.
She hopes they do not see war.
She says something else
which is not translated
that makes her blow her nose.
Spy lady is moved to sniffle.
Schoolboy turns away.
I sit there like Johnny-dumbfuck
with my finger up my nose.

VIII

I excuse myself and go to the dining car.
It is crowded, but I get the last table.
There are no Americans
and English is not spoken.
I order white wine and look out the window
seeing only myself;
I wonder who the stranger is.

I am tired and in neutral.
The night train passes my life
and I do not recognize it.
I am disoriented and relax
to the rhythm of the ride.
Hell, we're all just passin' through.
And nobody's train stops at anything
except for what we believe.
The rest is just accident.
The only schedule is death.
I try not to think
(I hate it when I get this way.)
She enters the dining car alone.

She comes to join me like we are married.
I touch her hand in a dry friendship
and would return to my brooding,
but she takes out a pen and notepaper.
She struggles with it—
I AM JUST HAUSFRAU
BUT LOVE WORLD IN PEACE.

I just look at her
and see her sons playing behind her eyes.
I take her pen and pad and scribble,
ONE DAY, NO MORE WALL.
ONE DAY OUR CHILDREN WILL MEET.
THEY WILL KNOW WHAT TO SAY TO
        EACH OTHER.
THAT IS THE DAY PEACE BEGINS.

She starts to cry softly and says,
"Hope and pray."
(When in hell did she learn to say that?)

67

I don't know why I do it,
but I reach inside my front pocket
and give her a U.S. dollar bill,
"Bet ya' a buck," I say.

She sniffles and finds a paper mark.
With an almost smile,
she stuffs it in my shirt,
"Bet ya'," she mimics.

And the most beautiful woman in the world
places her hand on mine,
"My name is Marion," she struggles,
and turns toward the window.

Our eyes meet in the infinity of reflection;
our minds watching our children
doing somersaults in a world without walls.

BACK TO THE BOSOM

It has been over one hundred years
since any of my family has breathed
Ukrainian air.
It smells like South Philly
with a taste of Chernobyl fallout.
I have no sense of glasnost
nor of fresh vegetables.

The Ukraine.
Under the czars they export food.
Under the communists they import it.
Either way, they eat each other.

Odessa.
The birthplace of my Russian grandfather.
The deathplace of the rest of his family.
His father was the czar's chief forester,
a giant of a man with red hair and a gentle voice.
The cossacks chop his family into toothpicks.

Grandfather is thrown
from a burning loft
by his mother's hand.
A sack of rubles
(sent with a prayer)
is thrown after him.
"Run. Run with God!"

He runs through the night fields
and into the frontier
the screams of cattle in his ears.

Grandfather stows away to America
on a German ship,
sells pencils at age eleven,
drives a Rolls at forty.
In '29 he works as a janitor
in the building he used to own;
tells me when he is an old man
a Russian proverb,
"Even if they should throw shit
in his face when he is down,
still he will get up."

I wonder
what I will tell
my grandchildren
(there are no American proverbs;
only one-liners).
Maybe, I will invent one for myself—
"Even if they should throw whipped cream
on his Armani suit, still he will be angry
that others have shit to eat."

I am not my grandfather—
I have, not yet, been cut down.
I am a man with the bark on.
I do five hundred push-ups a day
three hundred sit-ups,
smoke four packs of cigarettes,
drink a quart of anything
and think each day
while loving life,
this is a good day to die.

GREATCOAT AND THE GRANDMASTER

. . . it is bitterly cold,
there is no food on the train.
The latrine smells like a cattle car.
Rules are printed everywhere
in all languages except English.

I sit in my compartment
rolling to the rhythm of adventure.
I fall asleep crossing the "frontier"
and dream of a white-whiskered
gypsy woman riding an oxcart
under a Transylvanian moon
and wake to the kick of a border guard
who scratches at my passport picture
like he is digging my grave.
He does not guess that I could kill him
with the two practiced fingers
I use instead to make the sign of the cross.
It amuses me that he looks like
a uniformed member of the Addams Family.

The lady attendant brings me "chea."
I hate tea.
It is steaming and good.
I think my cold is now pneumonia.
She shows me how to convert
my seat into a bed.
I offer her the last of my cognac.
She points to her badge.

She looks like
an overweight Pete Rose in drag.
Her bosom could suckle Japan
and her smile
(when she sips the cognac)
is like morning in Georgia.
I like her very much.
She straightens her tie,
taps her badge
and laughs into the corridor.

In minutes, I step outside.
I see him in a bathrobe.
A professional traveler
brooding out a window.
I wonder why he does not stay
in his compartment.

He speaks English.
A tall, thin intellectual
with spectacles
and an uncanny intensity of focus.
It is like standing under a searchlight.
His mind hurts my eyes.

He comments about my health
and offers me something hot
in his berth.
I accept.
It is borscht from a thermos.
It warms me to eat beet soup
with a Russian.

I go to my place and retrieve Hungarian brandy
and a tin of Yugoslavian ham.

We make a party and talk.
We speak of glasnost and perestroika,
of Berlin of Rome
of art and of history.

I wax philosophical and quote Tarrasch
the old Grandmaster chessplayer,
"Chess, like poetry, like love,
has the power to make men happy."
He looks at me hard. It makes me wince.
He tells me his name;
he is an International Grandmaster chessplayer.

I cannot breathe. My eyes fill.
I begin to cry. He is confused.
Startled, as if I were having
a heart attack.
I am too overwhelmed to speak.
He says, "You know chess?"
I struggle, forcing up a smile,
"Just enough to know you are a hero."

I cannot tell him that in this world
I respect only children,
three-legged dogs, dead poets
and living Grandmasters.
I tell him instead a simple truth,
"Meeting you is the finest honor of my life."

The door opens abruptly,
a large, handsome man
says to me in English,
"Back to your compartment."
My heart leaps into action.

He is thirty-five
wears a greatcoat,
takes his work seriously,
like he is living a novel.
He is not a border guard.
He is something else.
He tells me to come outside.

Two men in uniform
sweep past us and into my compartment.
They search it roughly, thoroughly;
worry it, like dogs at a bone.
I am mildly amused.
I take out a Camel;
he tells me curtly,
no smoking.
I light up,
hand him my DuPont lighter;
it sits heavy in his hand
like a Cadillac on a dirt road.
I ask how many rubles
is 400 American dollars?
(fuck you, bureaucrat.)
He gets the message,
says nothing as I smoke.
(Those without things
are afraid of things.)

The Grandmaster
sticks his wise head out the door,
I smile at him and raise my hand,
he averts his eyes and disappears.
No wonder the best he played
Spassky and Karpov
was a "draw."

In "real-life"
if everybody plays it safe,
everybody dies.
No proverb, just truth.

We go back into my compartment.
It is a mess.
"Greatcoat" picks up a copy
of one of my books and asks,
"Who writes this shit for you?"
Bells go off in my head.
This asshole knows *me*.
This is not a perfunctory check.
This is *personal*.

I separate from myself,
run down the dark alleys of my life
hollering for that ice-cold, bad ass
in me who saves my shit in hard times.

I feel him step out of a dark doorway,
calm and confident, feel that smooth voice
inside me say, real easy-like,
"I'm here, pretty poet. Not to worry,
I'll handle this. This fuck is nothin'."
This persona steps around me and faces
"Greatcoat."

I sit back in the chair, cross my legs.
"What gave you the problem with it, syntax?"

His eyes get angry. His face does not move.
"Why do you visit only small towns.
Why do you come here at all?"

"My visa application says 'tourist.'
My papers are in order
and unless you have the price of that book,
put it down;
it's got enough shit with it already."

Whatever else he is,
"Greatcoat" is a man without combat.
I light another cigarette.
He says, "You are staying
at the Chernomore hotel."
I do not respond.
My eyes are flat.
I know they are flat.
When such as he looks at me
my eyes go dead like a snake's.
I can be killed.
I cannot be intimidated.

He says, "When you get there,
stay in your room.
Someone will speak to you."

I say, "If it has a bar,
you can find me there.
If it has women,
knock before you enter."

The door to my compartment
is locked for an hour.
When it is opened I do not know it.
I step outside and try to open a window
forgetting they are always locked.

The chessplayer appears at my side.
I do not turn from the window and say,
"Bobby Fischer would eat you
for breakfast."
He resigns without a word.

I think at that moment
I would give anything
to be eating a giant hotdog
in Dodger Stadium. . . .

NO MILK FOR A POET

It is in his eyes. It always is.
It is not something the eyes have.
It is something that is gone from them.
I say, "Afghansti?"

The bartender's eyes flame.
He pushes back from the bar,
elbows locked.
He looks at me like we will fight.
He drops one arm, swings away from me
pivoting like on a gate.
I think he is going to grab a weapon.
I do not change my position,
point to myself with my glass.
"Vietnam."
He folds into his outstretched arm
like it is rubber against the bar.
He shakes his head slowly
as if to bring color to his eyes.
He stands up, comes to me
like a wounded lion—
young, strong and in pain.
"I speak not so good English."

I say tiredly, "You are my brother
we do not need the words."
I throw a twenty on the bar.
"Drink with me."
He brings a bottle of Hennessey
from out a drawer near the register.
He pours us two shot glasses,

takes the twenty and stuffs it
in my open bag.

He raises the glass and says
something loud in Russian.
I sense the quiet behind us.

The Libyans are staring.
The bartender is waiting
for me to drink.
"What do we toast? What did you say?"
"The ones who not come home."
It is a good toast.
We shoot it down.

His name is Sergei.
Before the war he was a merchant seaman.
Picked up some English here and there.
Would love, "Who knows, these days
anything possible," to live in Italy.
Says that three years ago
he would not say even that.
But with this new man
we can start to talk.

He points to the TV.
A man is standing next to the wheel
of a farm machine which looks like
a mechanical dinosaur. A flesh-eater.
The wheel is at least eight foot tall.
The man is smiling.

My "brother" says to me,
"Gorbachev must first deal

with those pieces of shit.
Is real problem."

He walks to the TV and shuts it off.

He does another shooter of cognac.
"My friends die from Amerikanski guns."

I look at him, measure his sincerity,
the question he asks me:
"Twenty-five years ago, my best friend
in Vietnam was killed by an AK-47.
Soviet, no?"

Sergei shrugs his shoulders,
opens his palms and looks up,
searching for some truth;
finding none he looks down,
shakes his head and says,
"I do not know what to think—
these days none knows.
Good night, Captain."

I shake my head, too,
"Good night, Corporal."

It was not necessary
to speak of war
to know our ranks.
This man and I
do not know who we are,
but we know who we were.
It is not much,
but it is a beginning.
We are brothers.

THE SAME MAN AS I AM

The Benthanh Hotel, Ho Chi Minh City, 1989

It is the same place.
I am the same man.
Everything is changed.
Nothing is different.

The pink-tipped, cold whiteness
pasted against the paper-blue sky
is a monument to indifference.
The old Rex Hotel stands immutable,
impervious, ultimately distant.
Looking up at it
and trying to reclaim it
from the renamed street
is like sucking at a dead woman's breast.

Before 1975,
the war raged
the traffic snarled
the people suffered.
In the square outside the front doors
a heavy granite statue stood
commemorating the South Vietnamese
fighting man.

After 1975,
the war is over
yet there is no peace.
The city is now a bicycle kingdom—
there is no air pollution,

but there is little money
and almost no medicine.
The people suffer.
In the square outside the hotel,
a stunted palm tree
with a commemorative peace plaque
struggles under the sun
of the people's victory.

There is no parking for cycilos
on the street before the hotel.
The fine for the driver
is the equivalent of one month's wages
or an indeterminate jail sentence.
When I get to the curb my cycilo is there.
The driver has become my friend.

Two days before,
I am in a government van
parked outside the chained gates
of a walled fortress.
An official guest house for VIPs.
It is rumored, during the war
it was a "safe" house for transient POWs.

I wonder how I can sleep in such a place
my first night back in Vietnam.
I stare at nothing on the street,
but the movement of the bicycles.
My instincts notice something is wrong.
The same, empty cycilo has passed me twice.
I focus as the driver makes a slow circle
and comes up to my window from behind the van.

"Excuse me, Sir,"
he says in passable English,
"are you American?"
I nod with big-city distrust.
"Are you with the government?" I ask.
The man spits on the street.
I smile. "What do you want?"
I ask in Vietnamese,
and warn him I am at this moment
with government people.

He shakes his head slowly,
continues in English,
"I do not know—
just I am feeling as I pass—
something important about you.
I come back again and I know.
Something strange, here.
Sir, I think we are the same man."

What the fuck is this?
If this guy's a hustler,
he'd starve in New York.

Two hours later,
that first day back in Vietnam
after twenty-three years,
he says again over coffee,
"We are the same man."
I think to myself,
I am not so strong
nor half as good,
but I know what he means.

He says his name is Hai.
We are both fifty,
have two small children
the same ages,
fought on the same side
of the war, in the same area
at the same time.
We were both Army Captains.
We were both ambushed by the same
main-force VC battalion,
the 502.
Our fathers are Catholic.
Our mothers are dead.
We feel the same way
about old generals
and young women;
about small children
and big corporations.
We both love Vietnam.
In spite of everything.
Because of everything.

We hold hands in the street
as we speak of life.
I am worried: when I leave
there will be reprisals for him.
He sours his face and says.
"No problem. You are my friend—
two hundred percent."

I am not allowed to visit his home.
It is against the law.
We must stay only in public places.

After 1975,
Hai spent nine years in prison.
He is now "re-educated."
He works eighteen hours a day
pedaling a taxi-beast,
half rickshaw, half bicycle.
He earns the equivalent
of ten U.S. dollars a month.
It is enough for one lunch in Tokyo,
but not enough to own two shirts
in Ho Chi Minh City
or to feed the children first at mealtime.

The second night after we met,
I gave him 3200 U.S. dollars to hold
before I chased an old nightmare
up a riverfront back alley.
Hours later, at rat-scattering dawn,
I stepped back out of the puddles
and over the homeless
to this friend who earns 30¢ a day.
From under the rain-pelted poncho
at curbside, Hai's muffled voice spoke:
"I was right about you."
I shoved the money in my pants
and let him buy me breakfast.

Hai is my friend.
He makes me ashamed
and proud at the same time.

MARBLE MOUNTAIN

It is at that time of day
when the banana bats
leave the mahogany trees
and god stretches the thin yellow gauze
of eventide across the South China Sea,
that I enter the pale nether world
of the cathedral caves
within Marble Mountain.

Somewhere in New York
the gutter-hypes
are tying-off at the elbow
and just now
it is noontime anywhere in Romania
(a land without meat or cheese)
and any time of day
it is no time at all
in the shallow graves of young men
throughout the world
who are as old as they will ever get.

The incense vapors rise in a damp veil
fingering the endoskeletons
of million year old mastodons
and centuries old Buddhas in the walls.

On the America edge of the Pacific rim
my wife searches in consultation
for the childhood she never had,
six hundred kilometers to the south
the pickled embryos of mutated babies

float in hospital jars
before the eyes of the defoliated world
they never saw
and everywhere while babies starve
and the high priests sing,
lovers pump pleasure
into the sunken bellies of desperate nights
while theoretical physicists
in air-conditioned watchtowers
invent god for by-lined publication.

Marble Mountain.
There were five of them.
The Vietnamese called them
The Colors Mountains.
Iron, wood, stone, earth and fire.

During the war
young U.S. Marines painted their names
on the green and yellow marble teeth
of the mountain's face
and cranked their heavy guns
from atop its jungled head.

In the bowels of the mountain
the adolescent Viet Cong
softly scratched their names
into the black and hollow underbelly.

At night
(on either side of Marble Mountain)
mothers on both sides of the war
prayed to the one god to save their sons
from each other.

I follow my guide,
a former Viet Cong captain
(we call each other "dai ui"
with mutual respect and affection
and something like a little lingering dread),
across the dark, earthen floor of the mountain.

It is damp and cool
and the incense burns the back of my throat.
We pass through a shaft of mote-filled light
from a crack in the mountain ceiling
one hundred feet above our heads.

We are in the center of the cave
stripped to the waist
and glistening with sweat.

Eight monks in eight orange robes
sit on a single stone step
heads bowed almost to their laps.
Except for them we are alone.
I think that for them we are not here.
I think that for them we were never here.

Dai ui removes his shoes without a word.
I remove mine and follow him
to a hip-high crevice
at the base of the far wall.

From his left trousers pocket
he removes a red arm band
with yellow letters.
He touches it
with a kind of wonder and worship
and fixes it above his left elbow.

He smiles sheepishly up at me
as he goes to his knee
before the small black crack
in time and place
and I know that he is "flying his colors."

Out of respect for his brothers
I bow my head to his memory of them
and scream in my balls
for my own brothers.

He breathes quickly and deeply
and with the deftness of practice
takes a firm handhold
at what I know is an exact angle of entry
into the blackness.

"Mot phuc" I cry.
One minute, dai ui.
I am carrying an Italian handbag
with a shoulder strap.
Quickly I place it on the earth
and remove a smaller one with a hand strap.

From an inside zipper compartment
two metal miniatures jump into my hand.
My lapel pins.
The CIB—the Combat Infantryman's Badge—
and my silver parachutist's wings.
I stab them into my shorts.

The dai ui's eyes narrow and then widen.
He smiles broadly,
ant then his face goes blank—
flat like death—

and he nods his head
in the slowest movement I have ever dreamed.

He taps his arm band and says, "Phai di."
We go.
We disappear into the wall within. . . .

That night on China Beach
we two veterans of one lousy war
hold hands and walk ankle deep in the surf
beneath the Southern Cross.

We speak of our young children
as only two old men
with small children can.
Knowing that for us
life has offered a second chance
(knowing we will never know why).

And knowing too,
that this time we will not dance.
This time, we will teach the music.

Part IV

GOING FULL CIRCLE

In my personal journey from the experience of war to the commitment to peace, I have traveled far within myself and around the world. I have written three books: Johnny's Song, Warrior for Peace *and* The Human Being. *The completion of this trilogy brings me back to myself and finds me grateful to be "home" again. It was my intent (and always my hope) that my going full circle would encourage others to find their own way home.*

THE CASUALTY

From *Johnny's Song*, 1986

In the final end
we will have loved
more dreams than people;
given Time, some dreams come true—
most people prove false.
Truth, it seems, is an agreement
not long kept by friends and lovers;
it functions best between enemies
for whom the illusion of truth
is spirit for the first deceit.

These days,
like you, I am an expert in disbelief.
War in Vietnam and Peace in America
have imbued in us a God-like detachment;
a perceptual handicap,
which interdicts most lies.
For us,
neither the president,
not the emperor,
wears clothes.

And it remains the truest illusion of our war
that it is over;
the grandest delusion of our peace
that it is begun. . . .

It begins with simply this:
that each man goes to his war

as he goes to his love; alone.
And from neither does he return as before.
For love and war exist
at the edges of the human experience
and whether new-born or quick-dead,
life hangs in the balance.
Either way, man grapples with his universe
at the very limits of social restraint.
His cultural upbringing
too weak to govern
in the province of the darkness
and the dawn.

To survive in combat
a man must turn
from the teachings of other men
and come face to face with himself;
mano a mano.
In the dark,
instinct is a more perfect mirror
than reason.
And its first image
hurls the stone
which shatters the greatest lie
of his life;
that he is not alone.
For some it is a joy
to come to know such a man as he is.
For others, it is a nightmare
which recurs so long as he may live.

The world of the combat soldier
is a flat one
whose highest peak is mean survival
and whose lowest value

is the killing of his enemy.
It is a private world
of height without depth
from which can be viewed
the separate, fractured worlds
of comrades dying
(as from a galactic distance).
Strange, how close is a dead buddy;
how far is recalling his laughter.

It is a world
of unaccountable and indefinite season
where time is measured
by the Xing of the days
like the labored wall-scratchings
of condemned men.

It is a stereophonic world
of unspecified dimension
bordered on all sides by fear
and weathered by the tiny cloud puffs
of hope and prayer and dream
and a letter from home
which does not speak
of bills
or broken bones
or the unspeakable Death
of faithfulness.

War is a surrealistic penal colony
for young patriots of the real world
who, as sons of poor men,
must pay the price
for the believable myths
of national furors and private enterprise.

War as a social statement
has the depth of a slit trench at Argonne.
And echoes about as long
as it took the blood to dry at Hue.

When he wrestles at the edge
of his private, first-class world
where his least backward step
will plummet him into the cosmic promise
of his belief system,
each man knows
that in this, his final battle,
he fights neither for glory nor justice,
not for wealth
nor a cushioned seat
in the Kingdom of Heaven.
Not for country. Not for freedom.
He fights for the approval of his loved ones.
And he fights for his life.

If honor is to light the way to his Maker
it burns most brightly
when he sacrifices his life
for another.
In that gesture, humanity survives war.
And Peace clings
by a desperate finger
to a belt loop
of the stern, and long-striding History
of mankind
marching inexorably
toward some never-to-be-printed,
final date.

The combat veteran of Vietnam
lived in a world
where medals occasionally pinned themselves
on donkeys
and the green disappeared from the trees—
attacked by the one word in his language
which refused to rhyme;
Orange.
Years later,
it would bleach the rainbows
from his children's eyes
and then, nothing rhymed
(not even God)
and least of all, DOW.

The combat trooper searched to destroy.
In the end,
as a veteran,
he searched only to understand.
In Vietnam he looked for a reason.
And found none.
At home he looked for approval
and found none.
From the million, separate ledges
of his lonely worlds,
he jumped.
One
at
a
time
like lemmings into the sea.

Today,
many Vietnam vets
still hang

suspended
under
the floating shelves of their former worlds—
each by a single strand of sanity
more narrow than a window-washer's rope,
oscillating slowly into middle age
as from a madman's drool.
His family watches
from a window
ten stories
higher than the moon
unable to reach him
unable to understand him
unable to be unable
anymore.

The veteran swings between
murder   and   suicide.
His journey is the plain geometry
of conscience;
a pendulum's arc
tracing across the face of the sky
a child's smile
which asks the unspoken question,
"Who speaks for the little ones?"

. . . Well, remember those yuk-yuk,
backslapping, Brylcreem days
of the gridiron club meetings?
(What world was that?)
Those dreamy, green-tinted afternoons
when the giggles
of the future wives of America
floated through our windows
as they practiced the cheers

which would send us against
our dreaded, hated enemies next Saturday.
And the Saturday after that.
Bringing our enemies with it.
Strange, nobody seemed to notice
how after the first kickoff
the ambulance
would quietly pull behind the bleachers
(maybe it was bad luck to mention it).
God were we set up!
Women, cheers, uniforms, decorations,
parades, proud parents AND
the National Anthem!
What a life! When we were seventeen.

When we were eighteen
in Vietnam
only the ambulance showed up.
And when we got back home
somebody'd moved the town . . .

Well, maybe it didn't work.
But still it was a good dream.
A good way of life.
And so, we need another dream, that's all.
Hell, the one thing all suicides
have in common
is that each has lost his sense of humor.
C'mon bro, would you really
rather have been upstairs
in that airless room
(with the closed transom)
discussing the amount of sodium
on the back of a 2¢ King Louis
with the nerds of the stamp club?

Or been with us—fast and loose—
at street level
where the rubber meets the road?
At gut level, where a man meets a man?
Shit. C'mon bro, it's me you're talkin' to.
Shit.
Didn't lose any wars WE were in.
Didn't break any dreams WE believed.
Snap out of it, bro! Hear me!
We didn't lose anybody's fuckin' war.
We kicked ass!
We didn't break anybody's mutha fuckin' dream.
WE BOUGHT IT!!
Shit.
It was THEM.
THEY pulled out on US.
The moral equivalent of desertion
under fire.
The country didn't confuse the warrior
with the war.
They knew who we were.
It's themselves they loathe
and tried to avoid.
We merely remind them
of who they really are—
of their lack of courage:
moral and physical.
It takes strength to believe
and balls to put it on the line—
we had both.
They had neither.
And there's no such thing as benign envy.

But you know what?
After all the stories are told

and all the seas are salt,
it was you and me, bro,
who caught the fish;
who cut the fish.
We, the men;
ours, the dream.
Because we were together, we were strong.
And can be again!

We pulled ourselves out of the jungle mud
one buddy at a time.
And we can pull ourselves
out of this shit, too
(if we pull for each other).

You know,
I'll bet if the families of our brothers
killed-in-action
could sign a petition
charging each combat veteran of Vietnam
to live his life
as if he were living for two,
half of us would be on top of the world
by tomorrow afternoon!

A man may fight for his life
on a personal level,
but when he loves,
he does so for all mankind.
When we had no other reason to fight
in Vietnam
we fought for each other.
Today, in America,
it's still a good reason
to keep fighting.

Where once we saved each other
from death,
now we have the chance to save each other
for life!

Hey! bro,
when we're over the top?
Whadya say?
We fix the place up a little
for the kids, ya know?
Tell 'em a dream
they can make come true.
An' then jez hunker down
to watch 'em grow.

. . . and let no grim, graybeard of a god
speak again to us of glory
by bodycount.

THIS TIME, A WARRIOR FOR PEACE

From *Warrior for Peace*, 1988

Somewhere,
in the sad past
of each man alone,
is a woman
a song
a war
which if put to music
would be strings and harp,
symbols and cannon
for Maestro Toscanini
orchestrating spring
in each man's soul.

There,
seated in the balcony
of each man's sense
of what might have been,
is the memory
of a young man
with sad eyes,
hearing "no"
from a lover
who would have made
all the difference.

Now
(music aside)
he huffs and puffs

in the middle-aged city
of his choking dreams,
pulling on a waistline
too big for Levi's
and sees life through eyes
the color of faded denim—
sandpapered smooth as water
by the truth of her absence.

Tomorrow waits;
a buzzard on a signpost
with his name. . . .

One street over, maybe,
he might have lived, who knows?
Forever? And why not?
With a girl who fit
as tight as his imagination,
never got a head cold
or had a daughter
who needed braces.

And he wonders this fine day,
sitting on a spiritual knoll
somewhere on the bright side
of Venus
(and the dark side of youth)
just how far behind him
was that promise
of what might have been.
And what if he refused to budge
a galactic inch from here & now?

Could her Time catch up
on some parabolic line

from when they first said hello?
And would she this time say "yes"?

Ah, who knows how many tries
a happy man has had at life?

It is possible that each man's song
travels across the universe
like a musical rainbow,
arched in the harmonics of joy,
calling the cosmic matter
of his unborn children.

Well,
when with what years bring,
this poet goes the way of all dreams,
his song will still travel
until mathematics is displaced
by providence.
And still I will wait. And I will call.
And I will wonder.
But not of her.
And not of my children.

I will wonder of war.
And of the sons and daughters
of my enemy
whose real and separate worlds I broke;
ultimately and infinitely
in the rude finality of senseless Death.

When we kill a dreamer,
we bury alive
ten thousand dreams
and all his unborn children.

In this age of nuclear weapons
there is not enough world
to dig so deep a hole.

Even now,
on nights too real for sleep,
I can feel the human voices
of those aborted dreams
from deep within me—
and far, far out there.

And so I speak with them,
"Do re me fa so la ti do."
And then, I do not move.
I do not breathe.
I lift my chin to heaven
and listen in my heart
to their music—
knowing it will never,
never
be.
Oh, war. war. war.
There are casualties taken
on both sides of life.
We come from nonexistence.
We go to oblivion.
And war denies us
the middle worth living.

In my sad past
when I was still young,
I came home from war, alone,
my soul an unhung murderer.

One dark night
it stepped heavily
on the trapdoor of my guilt
and decorously hanged itself.

I pray it has found peace
away from me.
Perhaps, even now
it is grandfather
to the unborn dreams
of several particular rice farmers
I knew years ago
(and killed before I ever met).

These days,
the rest of me
is less agreeable
to romance and to war.
I am hard at work
making tomorrow come true
for the children
who have (thus far) survived.

I am a warrior for peace.
And not a gentle man.

UNCLE HO

Of nature the ancients loved to sing the charms:
Moon and flowers, snow and wind, mist hills and streams.
But in our days poems should contain verses of steel,
and poets should form a front line for attack.
>   —Ho Chi Minh
>   Jingxi Prison
>   Guangxi Province, China
>   August, 1942

I came to Hanoi to set flowers on your grave
and to pay respect to your sons and daughters.
I did so as a free man who loves life fully
and would rather die than live in bondage.

During the war I knew you as a nationalist.
Even when I killed your countrymen for mine
I never believed I was fighting communism.
One afternoon, far to the south, in 1966,
I visited you father's grave in Cao Lanh.
You were still alive then and the war raged.
Is there another American who visited you both?
Even that I did for me, not for you. Respect.

Without respect, there is nothing. Nothing—
but the empty days of waiting for Something.
Respect is the good mother of mutuality.
It begins with self and cannot end at others.

If I have enemies left alive in your country
they are those who do not love it as you did.
If there are dreams left for me in this life
they are the ones you and I shared all along—

the simple dreams of children growing strong
not fearing the madman's yoke or hangman's rope.

Like you,
I have seen the suffering in Harlem,
the duplicity of Paris,
the brutality of Moscow,
and the needless suffering
of your beloved Hanoi.

I, too, have traveled too far
to believe in miracles.
But having come this far,
I still believe in us—
you and me and all the others
who are simply human beings.
The greatness of you
was that you knew who you were.

I know you did not wish
a concrete monument to mark you.
Last year your final will was read
to your countrymen—
you asked to be cremated
and your ashes set in an urn
beneath the bamboo house
you chose over the mansion.
You wished that small children
would bring bamboo shoots
to be planted over you,
that life would grow about you.
Instead, the Soviets treated you
like a Muscovite hero.

I pray for you that one day
they will let you rest in peace
instead of lit-up in a glass cage
to lie forever in state.

I have left a little present
for us both near your home.
Something special
I have carried with me for many years.
A little rag doll
which belonged to a flower of Vietnam.
I hope this day,
not on this earth,
you and she are one.
That you will chase
the black and white clouds together
and hold hands as the Little Bear
dances over the Red River.

—*Steve Mason*
Hanoi, Vietnam
Bastille Day
1989